Usborne
Sticker Dollies
Unicorn Rescue

Zanna Davidson

Illustrated by Heather Burns
Cover illustration by Antonia Miller

Use the stickers to dress the Dolls on the 'Meet the Dolls' pages

Meet the Magic Dolls

Grace, Lily and Holly are the 'Magic Dolls'.
They care for the magical creatures, from
unicorns to fairies and mermaids, that live
on the Enchanted Isle.

Grace

is fascinated by all
magical creatures.
She reads books on
how to care for them
and spends as much
time as she can on
the Enchanted Isle.

Use the stickers to dress the Dolls

Lily

has a passion for flowers and fairies. She is brilliant at healing magical creatures with her herbs and flower potions.

Holly

has a special relationship with the trees and woodland creatures in the Spellwood. She also loves the mermaids that live by the Sparkling Shore.

Dolly Town

The Magic Dolls live in Honeysuckle Cottage, in Dolly Town, home to all the Dolls. The Dolls work in teams to help those in trouble and are the very best at what they do, whether that's fashion design, ice skating or puppy training. Each day brings with it an exciting new adventure…

The **Shooting Star** train whisks the Dolls away on their missions.

The Dolls love to celebrate at the **Cupcake Café.**

Madame Coco's Costume Emporium has everything the Dolls might need.

Rose Theatre

Animal Sanctuary

Bluebell Bookshop

Evergreen Sports Arena

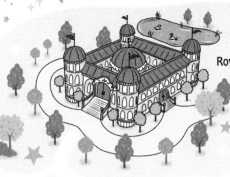

Royal Palace

Heartbeat
Dance Academy

Palm Tree
lm Studios

Fashion Design
Studio

Mission Control Centre
lets the Dolls know
who's in trouble and
where to go.

Pop Star
Stadium

Silver Sparkles
Skating Rink

Strawberry
Lane Stables

Honeysuckle Cottage
is home to the Magic Dolls.

HONEYSUCKLE
COTTAGE

Chapter One

Spring Cleaning

The Magic Dolls had decided that today would be the perfect day to spring clean Honeysuckle Cottage.

"Let's start with the library," said Grace. "All our books about magical creatures are in a terrible muddle."

"Then we could make a start on the potion room," added Lily. "I need to make up fresh batches of all my flower potions."

"And after that," said Holly, "let's treat ourselves to hot chocolate at the Cupcake Café!"

The Magic Dolls began pulling books from the shelves, sending sparkle dust pluming through the air.

The spring sunshine streamed in through the cottage window, and soon there were piles of books all over the library floor.

"I had no idea we had so many books," said Grace, sorting through the unicorn section. "I've found books on unicorn spells, what they eat, how to cure them, where to find them… But I can't find my *Guide to Unicorns* anywhere."

"What does it look like?"
asked Lily.

"It has a beautiful silver cover,"
said Grace.

"And, inside, there are pictures
of all the different kinds of unicorn
– from weather unicorns to frost
unicorns to forest unicorns…"

"Perhaps you left it behind on your last trip to the Enchanted Isle?" suggested Holly.

But before Grace could reply, the Dolls' watches began to flash.

Grace hurried over to the table and picked up her sparkly-cased screen.

MISSION CONTROL here!
Are the Magic Dolls there?

"We're all here," said Grace, tapping the star symbol on her screen. "What's happening?"

There's TROUBLE on the Enchanted Isle. A unicorn is charging through the Spellwood, scaring the other creatures in the wood, from the fairy rabbits to the mice and hedgehogs. She's trampling down flowers and destroying the Fairy Ring. We think she's frightened, but we don't know why.

"Oh no," said Grace. "But what about the fairies? They usually care for the unicorns. Haven't they been able to catch her?"

"They're all away," said Mission Control.

"Of course!" said Lily. "They're off collecting spring flowers for their spells."

"So it's up to us," said Holly. "We'll have to act fast. The unicorn could hurt the other creatures in the Spellwood."

"Or herself," said Grace. "A frightened unicorn can be dangerous, but we must rescue her."

Lily nodded in agreement. "Mission Control," she said. "Send through the mission details! We'll come right away!"

"Mission details coming through now," announced Mission Control, and the next moment a map flashed up on Grace's screen, along with a picture of the frightened unicorn.

MISSION LOCATION:

The Enchanted Isle

Fairy Palace

Fairy Ring

Silver Stream

Spellwood
X

Unicorn last seen here

Pixie Meadows

Unicorn Rescue Mission

Unicorn facts:

Unicorns are very shy creatures.

Unicorn wings are gossamer-light,
but they are strong fliers.

Look for unicorns by silver
streams and in woodland glades.

Always approach a
frightened unicorn with care.

Chapter Two

How to Catch a Unicorn

"Let's work out exactly what we need to take," said Lily, getting out a pen and paper so she could write a list.

"Ooh! I know just the book to help us," said Grace, pulling one out from her pile.

"Here we go," she said, turning

the pages until she reached the
chapter she needed. "How to
approach a frightened unicorn..."

HOW TO APPROACH A FRIGHTENED UNICORN

1 Dress in clothes that blend in with the forest.

2 Play a lilting tune on a silver flute. This can help calm a frightened unicorn.

3 Chime a silver bell three times. This will let the unicorn know you come in peace.

4 Approach slowly so as not to startle. Unicorns are shy, sensitive creatures.

5 Carry a calming flower potion. The scent will soothe an anxious unicorn.

6 Take a rope woven from rushes to place carefully around the unicorn's neck.

7 Speak softly.

"I'll fetch my silver bell and flute," said Grace, hurrying through to her study. "And I'll quickly weave a rope…"

"I think I have a calming flower potion," said Lily, going through to her potion room.

"Ah! Here it is!" she said.

Lily pulled down
a little glass bottle,
only to discover it
was almost empty.

She studied the flower potion book, lying open on the table, and began turning the thick, creamy pages.

Flower calming potion

Works well on unicorns, trolls and small dragons. (Avoid giving to pixies, as it seems to have the opposite effect.)

Two drops of rose hip syrup

Rose Hip Syrup

Five daisy petals

Three daydream
leaves

One stalk
of lavender

Four sweet peas

A sprinkling
of sparkle dust

Lemon balm

Mix well and shake.

Holly popped her head round the door as Lily set to work. "I've just thought," she said. "If the unicorn is rampaging through the forest, there might be trees that are hurt as well. I'd better take one of your healing potions for enchanted trees."

At last, the Magic Dolls were
ready. Lily checked her list.

"We've got everything," she said.

"Excellent," replied Grace.
"Next stop, Madame Coco's
Costume Emporium."

We need to
find clothes
that will help us
blend in with
the forest.

As they left Honeysuckle
Cottage, Lily cast one last glance
at the higgledy-piggledy mess on
the library floor. "The spring
cleaning will just have to wait," she
said, firmly closing the front door.
"This is much more important…"

Chapter Three

Flower Garlands and Silver Cloaks

Outside, it was a beautiful spring day. Dolly Town seemed to sparkle in the morning sunshine. Birds were singing on the street corners and fluffy white clouds scudded across the sky.

"It's strange to think that

somewhere out there is a very frightened unicorn," said Grace. "I do hope we're able to find her."

But however anxious she felt, Grace couldn't help a little thrill of delight as they approached Madame Coco's. Its beautiful arched brickwork gleamed in the sunshine, the flags fluttered in the breeze, and as usual, the windows gave a tantalising glimpse of all the wonderful clothes inside.

The Dolls pushed through the revolving door and made their

Floor 9
Theatre costumes

Floor 8
Dance Outfits and
Accessories

Floor 7
Magical Dept. Floor

Floor 6
Royal Dept. Floor

Floor 5
Ballet Costumes &
Accessories

Floor 4
Pop Star &
Movie Star Outfits

Floor 3
Animal Rescue
Outfits & Equipment

Floor 2
Sports Cloth

Floor 1
Horse Ridin
and Acce

Ground Flo
Wedding &

way to the famous
glass elevator.

"Where would
you like to go
today?" asked Jasper,
the lift attendant,
looking as smart as
ever in his uniform.

Floor number seven,
please Jasper.

Jasper pressed the number for the Magical Department Floor. At once, the doors closed and the lift glided up and up, coming to a stop with a gentle

TING!

When the doors opened again, the Dolls stepped out into an airy room that seemed filled somehow with the soft green light of the forest.

Beautiful clothes hung from cut-out trees and the room was full of everything the Dolls could need to look after magical creatures.

There were fairy cloaks and mermaid combs, winter coats for unicorns and special flowers for decorating their manes and tails.

"Oh look!" said Lily. "Here are the pixie hats we ordered last time!"

"Aren't they lovely?" said a voice,

and the Dolls turned to see Madame Coco gliding over to greet them. "Hello Lily, Grace, Holly," she said, smiling at each of them in turn.

How can I help you today?

Grace showed Madame Coco the picture of the unicorn on her screen. "This frightened unicorn is on the loose in the Spellwood," she explained.

"We have to catch her before she does any more damage, or hurts herself. The fairies are away right now, so it's all down to us. It's very important we wear the right clothes, so we don't scare the unicorn."

"Of course," said Madame Coco. "Three outfits coming up…"

She whirled around the shop, her eyes flicking expertly over the shelves as she picked out a skirt here, a flower garland there…

"Holly," she said, "I've chosen your outfit…"

Holly's clothes

A top made from emerald green leaves

A leaf garland with ruby red berries

A skirt with leaf-shaped pleats

Felt boots wrapped round with vines

Lily's clothes

A flower hair decoration

A soft lilac top

A skirt embroidered with flowers

Lilac slippers

"Grace, you'll need something special to wear," Madame Coco went on. "With your unicorn knowledge, you must be the one to catch the unicorn."

Grace's clothes

Star hair clips

A silver necklace

Silver shoes to match

A dress that sparkles as silvery-white as a unicorn's coat

"Thank you. They're beautiful," said Grace.

The Dolls stepped into the changing rooms…

Moments later, they were dressed and ready for their mission.

"You look like sprites from the forest," said Madame Coco, clapping her hands in delight. "Perfect clothes for catching a unicorn."

48

Last of all, Madame Coco handed each of them a soft silver cloak, the colour of birch bark. "These should keep you warm," she said. "You never know what will happen with the weather on the Enchanted Isle."

"Thank you, Madame Coco," said Holly, as they waved goodbye, "for all your help."

"Good luck!" Madame Coco called after them.

The elevator
whizzed back
down

TING!

and soon they
were standing
again on the
sunny street.

"Time to
catch the
Shooting Star,"
said Lily, tapping
her watch.

A moment later,
the magical train drew up
in a cloud of glittering dust.

"Where would you like to go?"
asked Sienna, the train driver.

"The Spellwood, on the
Enchanted Isle, please," said Lily.

"Step aboard!" said Sienna.

The train pulled away in
another burst of sparkles,
winding its way through
Dolly Town, and then out
through a dark tunnel,
glittering with lights.

Chapter Four

Into the Spellwood

The Shooting Star drew up at the very edge of the Enchanted Isle.

A sparkling sea lapped at the shore, dazzling rainbow birds flitted between the branches while little pixies peered out over the mossy green banks.

"I daren't go any further,"
said Sienna, "in case I disturb
the magical creatures. Is it okay
if I drop you here?"

"Of course," said Grace.
"We can follow the Silver
Stream into the Spellwood."

"Thank you," they called,
as Sienna began to pull away.

"Good luck with your
mission," Sienna replied.
"And watch out for the
weather…"

The Magic Dolls looked up to see huge grey clouds gathering above the Spellwood.

"That's strange," said Holly. "There are blue skies all around. Why would there be a storm cloud above the Spellwood?"

"Of course!" said Grace, thinking back. "Mission Control told us that the unicorn has a rainbow mane. That means she's a weather unicorn. Her moods have the power to change the weather."

If she's frightened or anxious, she could easily bring on a storm.

Grace glanced up again at the billowing clouds, which seemed to be growing darker by the minute. "That makes it even more important we find her and calm her down."

Without another word, the Dolls followed the Silver Stream into the Spellwood, each of them searching for signs of the unicorn.

As they went, Lily couldn't help but notice the beautiful wild flowers either side of the stream.

Lily longed to pick them, to make up fresh flower potions, but she knew the laws of the Enchanted Isle. No flowers could be picked without permission from the fairies, and they weren't there for her to ask them.

"Look!" Grace called out suddenly. "The unicorn must have passed this way. I can see trampled toadstools."

"And these trees have broken branches," said Holly, hurrying over to some young saplings.

She tended to them with her healing potion, while Grace searched for new signs.

"Oh!" she cried. "I've found a trail of hoof marks. It looks like the unicorn cut a path through these bushes."

The Magic Dolls walked on,
as quietly as they could. Then
suddenly, up ahead, without warning,
they saw the unicorn. She flashed
past them, silver-white, horn

lowered, as beautiful as a snowflake
on the wind.

Grace whipped out her flute, but
it was too late. A moment later, the
unicorn had vanished from sight.

"Where could she have gone?" asked Lily, looking this way and that.

"I can't see any sign of her now," said Holly. "And look – the storm's picking up."

A sharp wind had begun whistling through the trees, lashing at the branches. Rain began to fall from the sky in thick curtains.

The Magic Dolls pulled their cloaks around themselves. They had no choice but to carry on through the forest. From under the dripping branches, they could see the fairy rabbits and mice peeking up at them, their little faces anxious.

All around, the storm was starting to destroy the animals' woodland homes. The little streams were overflowing their banks, and moles were hurrying out of their flooded burrows. The creaking trees sounded as if they might fall to the ground at any moment.

Chapter Five
Silver Hoof Prints

G race took up her flute again and began to play. She hoped her book was right – they really needed help to find the unicorn.

At first she was worried that the sound would be

drowned out by the storm, but the flute had a magic of its own, and soon the tune was cascading through the forest.

"This way," said Holly.

"I think I've picked up her trail." She pointed to the downtrodden flowers on the woodland floor and the broken branches, which made a messy path through the trees.

Then Holly let out a gasp. "Up ahead," she whispered. "In the clearing... I think I see her!"

Lily and Grace peered through the trees to see a silver-white shape, right at the back of the clearing.

They began to walk slowly towards her. "At last," said Grace, putting away her flute. "We've found her."

The unicorn was standing very still, watching them warily, as if the slightest movement might startle her into running away again.

Slowly, carefully, the Magic Dolls moved closer towards her, while Holly began to chime the silver bell.

"This is it," Grace whispered to the others. "You two wait here. I'm going closer. I do hope I can win her trust..."

She tiptoed over the fallen
leaves, one arm outstretched,
talking softly to the unicorn
all the time.

"Don't worry, I promise
I won't hurt you," said
Grace, gently.

Behind her, Lily gently wafted her calming flower potion on the wind, and Grace could see it take effect. The unicorn's breathing slowed and she bowed her head.

Grace placed her hand on the unicorn's nose and began to stroke her mane.

Now that she was close to the unicorn, Grace could see the sparkling silver flecks in her white coat and the flowing colours in her mane and tail.

"She doesn't seem to be injured," Grace whispered to the others, as she gently placed the rope of woven rushes around the unicorn's neck.

"I think we should take her to the Fairy Palace. Then when the fairies return, we can check her over to see what's wrong. She must be frightened for a reason."

"Good idea," said Lily. "The Fairy Palace is west of here, where the island meets the sea."

She pointed towards the setting sun.

But as they led the unicorn
through the forest, Holly couldn't
help noticing that the storm wasn't
dying down. The branches of the
trees waved this way and that, and
the rain still cascaded from the sky.

The unicorn tossed her head, her eyes glancing round, as if she were looking for something.

"She's still upset," said Grace. "I just wish I knew what it was."

They hadn't gone far when Lily pointed to some little silver marks on the ground. "I wonder what these are?" she said, bending closer to look.

Oh! They're silver hoof prints!

"Now I understand," said Grace. "Only a baby unicorn leaves hoof prints like those. The weather unicorn must be looking for her foal. I don't think she's frightened for herself at all – she's frightened for her baby!"

As soon as the unicorn saw the silver hoof marks, she snorted and whickered, pawing at the ground in excitement.

"The tracks go this way!" said Grace, her eyes following the silvery trail, which led deeper

and deeper into the Spellwood.
They could all feel that the
unicorn's mood had changed.

She seemed much less frightened now, more determined. Ears pricked, she led the Dolls through the forest, always checking to see where the next hoof print lay.

Sometimes the trail would disappear for a while over hard ground or across a stream...

...but then the unicorn would find it again.

"I think she's picked up a scent," said Grace, seeing the unicorn stop and sniff the air.
The next moment, the unicorn threw back her head and let out a long, loud whinny.

Neighhh!

Then she charged forward,
moving so fast that the rope of
woven rushes slipped through
Grace's fingers.

The unicorn crashed through
a clump of bushes, the
Dolls running after.

When the Dolls caught up
with the unicorn, they gasped.
There, standing next to her, in
the middle of the Fairy Ring,
was a beautiful little unicorn
foal. Her coat was flecked with
silver, just like her mother's, and
she stared at them out of the
same anxious dark eyes.

Chapter Six

The Storm's End

"*Isn't she beautiful,*" whispered Holly, as they edged closer. The Dolls could see now that the little foal's horn was wedged in the twisted trunk of a tree.

Grace went over to her, carefully resting her hand on the foal's head. The mother unicorn looked on,

"We have to find a way to get her out," said Lily.

"But how?" wondered Grace.

"I have an idea!" said Holly, and she quickly began searching through her bag.

"I don't know if it will work, but it must be worth a try."

She pulled out her little glass bottle, filled with ointment to heal the enchanted trees.

"I could try rubbing some around the hole in the trunk. Then, with our help, the foal might be able to pull out her horn."

Grace stepped back to make way for Holly. "Oh I do hope it works," she said.

"I'll be very gentle," Holly whispered to the little foal.

She held up the glass bottle and, drip by drip, managed to pour some of the ointment into the hole in the trunk.

"Now, on the count of three," she said. "I'll hold onto the foal's horn and gently pull backwards. Grace, can you help push her chest?"

When the Magic Dolls were all in position, Lily called out. "One... two... *three!*"

There was a faint

POP!

and all at once, the
foal was free.

The foal's mother ran to her side, nuzzling her, drawing her close. Then the mother unicorn looked at Grace, deep into her eyes. Grace knew, without needing any words, that the unicorn was thanking her. The rain had stopped too.

Then together, the
mother and foal walked
away. The mother gave
one last look over her
shoulder, as if in farewell,
and they disappeared
from view.

Lily tapped her watch. "Mission accomplished!" she reported.

"Congratulations," replied Mission Control. "We'll ask Sienna to come for you."

"Time to go home," smiled Lily.

The Dolls wound their way back through the Spellwood, and out to where the sparkling waters lapped at the shore of the Enchanted Isle.

Holly looked up, to see the
storm clouds clearing.

"There!" cried Grace, pointing.
Above them, flying high, was the
unicorn and her foal, painting a
rainbow across the sky.

A moment later, the Shooting Star train drew up beside them, its cloud of glittering stars sparkling in the sunshine.

"Well done, Magic Dolls," said Sienna. "Where would

you like to go now?"

"We should really go back to Honeysuckle Cottage," said Holly, as the doors glided open. "We've still got all our spring cleaning to do."

"How about we do that *after* a cup of hot chocolate?" suggested Lily.

"I agree," laughed Grace. "Take us to the Cupcake Café, please Sienna. Hot chocolate here we come!"

The train sped away, leaving
the Enchanted Isle far behind.
Then they entered the tunnel,
flickering with tiny stars.

WHOOSH!

When they arived at the
Cupcake Café, the Magic Dolls
sat outside in the sunshine.

Holly blew on her hot
chocolate to cool it down, while
Lily was gazing in delight at her
swirling mound of whipped
cream.

"This is going to be *dee-licious*,"
said Grace, grinning, stirring the
marshmallows so they melted
into the thick chocolate.

But before any of them could take a sip, their Mission Control watches began to flash.

"Oh no!" said Grace. "I do hope the unicorn's not in trouble again."

She quickly tapped the star symbol on her watch.

"We're all here, Mission Control," she said. "What's happened? Is the unicorn okay?"

"Everything's fine," said Mission Control.

You ALL did a fantastic job. We just wanted to let you know that the fairies have come back from their trip to the islands across the sea. They're so grateful to you for rescuing the unicorn and her foal, that they've left a present for you at Honeysuckle Cottage.

"Oh how kind!" said Grace. "Thank you for letting us know!"

As soon as the Magic Dolls had finished their hot chocolates, they hurried home.

"I wonder what the present will be?" said Holly.

She was half-expecting a parcel on the doorstep, but there was nothing to be seen.

Lily opened the door and...

"Oh *wow!*" she cried. "The fairies have done our spring cleaning!"

She ran from room to room. "They've done the library! The kitchen..."

The whole cottage!

Every room was sparkling.

And best of all, on the kitchen table, were three presents – one for each of them.

"A collection of enchanted flowers," said Lily. "Just what I wanted! Now I can make up fresh flower potions."

"And they've given me more healing ointment for the trees!" said Holly, beaming. "What about you, Grace?"

118

Grace was clutching her present, hugging it to herself. "It couldn't be more perfect!" she said. "Look!" And she held out a book.

"And…" said Holly, "there's an invitation, too."

The Fairies invite the **Magic Dolls** to the **Spring Fairy Picnic** on the Sparkling Shore. Fairy Rose will meet you at the entrance to the Spellwood at 2pm.

"A Fairy Picnic!" said Lily.

"A perfect end to an exciting mission," said Grace. "I can't wait for the next one."

Then the Magic Dolls stood side by side, their arms around each other.

Magic Dolls forever!

The End

Join the **Magic Dolls**
on their next adventure in

Read on for a sneak peek…

T he Magic Dolls were
dancing around their cottage
in excitement. The fairies had
invited them all to a picnic on
the Enchanted Isle and, at last,
the day of the picnic had arrived.

"I've been looking forward to
this for so long," said Lily. "All the

fairies are going to be there – the
Flower Fairies and the Tree
Fairies, the Sky Fairies and the
Meadow Fairies…"

"I know!" agreed Holly. "I
can't wait!"

…Just then, there was a
whooshing sound and they all

turned to see three little silver bags
floating through the letter box.

"What's this?" wondered Grace.
"Oh!" she said, picking up one
of the bags. "There's a note.
These are from the fairies.
They've sent us tiny bags of
sparkle dust."

Dear **Lily**, **Holly** and **Grace**,
Please sprinkle this over
yourselves when you arrive on
the Enchanted Isle. You're in
for a magical surprise!

"How exciting!" said Holly. "I
wonder what the sparkle dust is for..?"

First published in 2020 by Usborne Publishing Ltd.,
Usborne House, 83-85 Saffron Hill, London EC1N 8RT, England.
usborne.com Copyright © 2020 Usborne Publishing Ltd. UKE